JESUS, THE LOST YEARS

JESUS, THE LOST YEARS

T.R. ANTHKO

CONTENTS

CHAPTER I

A Father's Trade

"Come, we will look for wood on the beach. Today is a good day. We shall see if a ship has wrecked on the beach. The tax collectors come in one week. We need to have goods to sell at the market so we may keep our place."

"Daniel, you will tend the mule and watch for guards and robbers today while Father and I collect what we can find."

"Oh Jesus, can't I help collect the wood? I am getting stronger."

"Be good and honor your father, my young miracles," their mother called to them as they departed.

"The guards have been vigilant since the northern people started appearing with exotic goods. Too many robbers have been trying to loot. We need you to protect the mule," Joseph instructed.

"Yes, father, I will honor you."

As the three made their way down to the sands of their small village, they could see a northerner ship docked. Men were pulling crushed wood from one edge of the ship's deck, then chipping chunks from the surface of the firm, flat tan sand. At the other end, men brought horses and wood onto the ship's remaining deck.

When Joseph, Jesus, and Daniel reached the beach, the men had already begun installing the new wood. The ship was almost fully patched. The soles of the trio's feed began to simmer through their thin leather-soled sandals as they made their way toward the blackened wood.

Suddenly appearing before them in the sand were two arrows as foreign shouts blistered their ears. The men from the ship were scaling down ropes and surrounding the wood with swords drawn.

"Father, we should leave. We can find different wood."

"No, Jesus, God tests us. We must have faith that he will provide. We shall see if we can negotiate for the wood."

"Yes, Jesus, we must honor our father and our God. They will protect us like they protected the great Daniel, after whom I am named."

"Daniel, untie the donkey," Joseph commanded. Daniel honored his father. Without letting his gaze stray from the wood or the men surrounding it, Joseph pointed at the wood and then at the donkey. An arrow whizzed through the air and stuck the donkey in its thigh. "Okay, they do not want the donkey. We can fix up the donkey later. She is strong."

"Father, maybe we should go. God will provide for us in all ways. We need to spare our donkey any more agony," Daniel rationalized. "We can find more wood along the beach down there."

No sooner were the words out of his mouth than four of the men grabbed Jesus and Daniel and bound them with rope. A man stepped away from the pile of wood. He pointed at the wood and then at Jesus and Daniel. Joseph had never in his life seen such magnificent and exotic black wood. It would easily fetch a premier price at the market. He could finally get out of debt and make a name for himself. Joseph prayed to God.

"My sons, God is testing you. You need to go with these men and learn where they are from. Learn how to trade with them and collect more of this wood. God will guide you and protect you. Do as I have instructed and honor your father. God has provided this wood for me and this test to see if your faith is steadfast." Joseph lost balance as he attempted to lift one of the planks. Blood gushed from his brow as ferocious laughter from the northern men pillaged the ears of all.

As Jesus and Daniel were dragged onto the ship, they could see their father continue to struggle to get the wood in the cart, blood now covering his face. Streaming from Daniel's eyes were tears that striped his cheeks.

"Calm, Daniel, we will see father again soon. We will repay the debt with our labor and return before the next planting season."A heavyset man cantered over and pointed at two crates. "We don't understand. We are bound," said Jesus as he lifted his arms to show the ropes. Slashing the ropes with a knife, the man pointed again. "Daniel, I think he wants us to sit."

The crates felt rough and cold through their thin garments. A metallic cup was placed before them as a fur sack poured water. The heavyset man in animal skins pointed at the cup, then he pointed at his mouth, and then at each of them.

"Daniel, take a drink and calm yourself. Many people have told me it takes two days to cross the sea. We won't be that far from home." As Daniel wiped his tears, the lines on his face smeared. Slowly raising the cup, he drank. He hadn't realized how thirsty he had become and drank all the water. It was such a small cup.

As he placed the cup back on the table. The man stood and shouted at the crew. They were working diligently to make the ship ready for the sea. Several men stopped working and dragged Daniel to the center of the deck. Jesus stood and tried to pull Daniel back.

"Jesus, help me. Help, please. What are they doing? Please make them stop," fear and panic swelled in his cries. Jesus began punching and kicking the men with no reaction. Jesus found a loose board on the deck. He bashed it into one crewman, then another, then the man who gave them water.

The man started shouting and pointing at Jesus. The crew bound Jesus to the ship's side and ensured he faced Daniel. Daniel had begun to pray. They stripped Daniel and placed his clothing in a container on the deck while two crewmen held Jesus's eyes open.

"Jesus, please make them stop. Please, what did I do? Why is God doing this? Please, please make them stop," Daniel was frantically shouting.

The man who had given them the water walked to Daniel as the other men held him down. He looked Jesus in the eyes as he slowly slid his sword through Daniel's throat. A high whine turned into a deep gurgle as Daniel's face contorted. The life in his eyes faded into glassy hollowness. The men drew their swords and began chopping Daniel into small pieces. A foot, a hand, four leg parts, Daniel's head, and all other parts severed. Daniel's blood and entrails sloshed back and forth with the motion of the waves. As Daniel's remains were pushed into the water, Jesus could see Joseph still loading the wood into the cart.

The men untied Jesus from the side of the ship and uncontrollably sobbed. His feet dragged against the knobby deck as they pulled him to the rear of the boat. They opened a hatch in the floor and then plopped Jesus's body into the hole.

Sobbing in the darkness, Jesus hardly noticed the water that rose to his torso.

"You need to calm yourself," a deep, heavily accented voice spoke.

"God, is that you?" Jesus heaved through the tears.

"Your god is not here. No god is here. You need to calm yourself before they do to you as was done to your brother."

"Who are you?"

"I have had many names, too many to remember. The name of my honor was lost many masters ago, but I am not your enemy."

"How long have you been on this boat? Where are you from?"

"I have only been on this boat a day or two before you. It is hard to tell now long when I cannot see the sun, the moon, or the stars. Listen to my story for comfort. Our words will be the only thing we hear in this place."

"Tell me, tell me your story," Jesus's breathing slowed as he wiped the snot from his face.

"I am from my Jia, my family place. It is far, far away in the east. We were attacked by the armies from the south and taken as slaves to Niagara. Niagara is a great city in a great empire. Never in my life had I imagined such a place with so many people and such large boats and markets. I worked for a farmer there who grew herbs for teas, potions, and elixirs. One day, he died. The empire seized the farm. I was sold to a wretched man. He would bring me to the ocean and beat me with a spiked whip if his gods did not provide enough fish. One day, in a place hotter than the sun, he had me unloading the fish for the market. I could see him getting upset with his god while speaking with someone. He grabbed his whip and began to whip the man and the woman with that man. The city guards grabbed my master and removed his whipping hand. Then the guards took all of his things, including me. We were all placed on a raised platform with many people crowding around. A guard pointed at one of the possessions and then screamed. The crowded market burst into an uproar with frantic hands extending money into the sky. Some men jumped to get their money higher, others climbed on things, and others shoved their way through the masses to the man. When the man pointed at me, I heard a camel drinking in the distance. Everyone was frozen like statues baked in the sun. A single man held money up and came to me and motioned for me to follow. His name was 'Timboola.' Timboola was kind to me. He gave me hay to sleep on, his scraps from meals, and didn't make me work during the hottest parts of the days. He helped teach me his language and the language we speak now. He was a nomad with great knowledge of herbs, spices, and rocks. We traveled up and down the Nile. He purchased me in Haifa. We traveled up and down the river, trading in many towns. We traveled to Alexandria a week ago. It wasn't our first time. Timboola fell ill this time. He had no choice but to trade me for herbs. Alexandria is such a big and amazing and dangerous and wonderful place. They say slaves are freed in Alexandria every day. Maybe someday we will return and be freed together, my new friend. These trade ships always return to every port they visit. Maybe we will return soon enough. But now you should get some rest. You will need your strength no matter how long we are here or what happens next."

"How can I rest? We are in the water."

"Lay against the side, right in the corner where the floor meets the ceiling. It is the driest there. Also, hold back your tears. You need to keep the water. You cannot drink this. It will make you very ill."

Jesus lay in silence. He couldn't stop replaying Daniel's final pleas nor how his face contorted. The darkness only provided a screen to watch the day's events unfold countless times. Then Jesus began to think of how he would tell his dear mother, Mary. How could he tell her such horrible things? What would Joseph tell mother? Jesus couldn't discern awake from sleeping, dead or alive, moving or lifeless. Fatigue overtook him and cemented his eyes shut despite his tremendous attempts at resistance.

CHAPTER II

Sailing the Unknown

"Come, you do not want to remain here when they close that door again. It is time to work."

The bright sky above the calm bay blinded Jesus as he emerged wet and shivering. He could hear distant shouting as fragrant smoke tickled his nostrils. A thud reverberated through the deck beside him, into his foot, and up his leg.

"Your eyes may need a moment to adjust; your arms do not. Start moving these boxes to the far side of the boat for unloading, whispered The Voice. "Can you feel the grooves in the wood beneath your feet?" Jesus nodded. "Good. Follow them for ten paces and stack these goods." The Voice grabbed Jesus's hand and led it to the first box.

Jesus fingered the top and side of the sun-weathered, gritty box. There was a thin lip on the edge he could hold. Jesus listened to the men taking on the deck as he shuffled his feet. His sight was slowly returning to crisp focus. He neither recognized the people who now surrounded him nor understood their language.

"How did you come to be on this boat?" Asked the men in red clothes adorned with dark brown, sun-weathered leather as their bronze helmets glinted. The question was simple, yet an apple grew in Jesus's throat as his mouth dried and tears welled. The response was prevented. "The crew says you are a slave traded for some old rotten wood. Are you from Alexandria?"

"My father lives in Tuttriam just north of Alexandria. I must work off his debt," Jesus managed. The group turned their attention to the boxes, inspecting the spices, oils, wines, and Daniel's clothes. Oh, poor Daniel. Jesus's face started to tighten, his jaw taught, as he clenched his hands.

"Don't," whispered The Voice. Jesus looked over at the most peculiar person he had ever seen. The Voice was a short man with wide eyes that were different and tilted. His sinewy frame was draped with a simple cloth with a winged serpent.

The men in helmets took two jugs of wine and then spoke to the crew as they pointed at two boxes they had nailed shut. Just then, one of the crew members pushed past Jesus and began running down the sliver that connected the boat to the cobblestone dock. The men in helmets yelled out. Arrows sliced through the air and sunk through the man's chest. Small blood-filled eruptions spewed from his back. The man's body crumpled and slowly tipped into the sea. The men in helmets pointed at the lifeless body and screamed at the crew. The body had already begun to stain the water. The men then picked three more bottles of wine and departed.

A crew member yelled at The Voice and struck both him and Jesus with a thin reed across the arms and back. The sting zapped across Jesus's skin and burned his muscles.

"Come, we must take these open boxes down there and create a shop." Jesus lifted a box and followed. "Be careful on this wood as it bows. The water is deep," whispered The Voice. A strange man had finished fishing the lifeless body out of the water with a grappling hook by the time all the boxes were unloaded. A cart filled with bloated and lifeless forms collected the recently departed vessel. A crew member begrudgingly provided the driver with a silver coin and then spat on the dead man.

"Put the contents on the lids like this," instructed The Voice as three crew members lazed behind them with wineskins.

The pink horizon faded into black as the final boxes were secured. Jesus's legs were burning jello; he could barely walk. Under the soft glow of a torch, a crew member pointed at the slave pair and then pointed to a place on the deck. The place was stained with the blood of Daniel. Jesus's eyes widened, his heart raced, and he felt cold as sweat formed on his brow.

"He wants us to sit. Be calm. It is almost time to rest," The Voice firmly grasped Jesus's wrist and pulled him to the deck with a thud. The crewman disappeared behind the cargo. They were befriended by the warm black Mediterranean night once more. As the glow began walking back to Jesus, he became aware that his face, arms, and legs were taut with the ocean salt and sweat. The torch threw two a burned chicken at the feet of The Voice.

"Here, eat. We do not get such feasts often. We must eat to keep our strength. Be quick," The Voice ripped a large chuck of the breast from the chicken and handed it to Jesus no quicker than he buried his face in the remains.

Jesus awoke below the deck to an unusual sight; sunlight permeated the space. The Voice silently swayed with the ship's rhythm. A hand appeared in the sunlight holding a cup. Jesus shrank away and hid behind The Voice. Then the hand disappeared. Great thudding started overhead, boards flexed, and dirt rained.

The Voice roused, "What is going on? Why is the door open?"

"They are going to kill us. There was the cup of death."

The hand with the cup reappeared in the sunlight. This time, it was accompanied by shouting.

"Come, they want us to come to learn. We must go." The Voice crawled into the light and climbed into the sun. Jesus wearily pursued, his eyes adjusting to the light more quickly that day.

The man who had slain Daniel was sitting on a box with bread and a cup. He pointed to the floor. The Voice and Jesus sat. The man raised the bread and spoke a strange sound.

The Voice echoed the word and then said, "bread." The same happened with the cup as it was filled with water. After several cycles, the man pointed at Jesus, held up the bread, and said the same sound. It was hard to concentrate with the burning of an empty stomach as sandpaper shredded his throat and tongue.

In a low, dry voice, Jesus slurred the words. The man repeated the words more slowly. Jesus tried again. The man's face turned red as he slowly repeated the words. Jesus tried again. Now leaning toward Jesus, he raised his voice while slowly repeating himself. Jesus took a deep breath, slowly tried to focus on every sound, and tried once more.

The man turned his attention to The Voice, who repeated the two words. It was Jesus's turn again. He repeated the two words more precisely this time. The man ripped the bread in half and gave each slave a piece. He then gave each man a wooden cup filled with water. He walked away. Two crew members sat watching the slaves.

Jesus could see the sun was behind the boat, with tall statuing land on both sides. Blackened skies lay ahead. The crew worked frantically along the deck. The door to Jesus's new abode closed with a heavy thud, sails lowered, anchor raised. Jesus's and The Voice's torso and shoulders were bound with rope to the ship's mast by the men guarding them.

The sea was violent, indiscriminately whipping the bodies of men with the salty brine. It rocked the boat from side to side, the top edge almost kissing the assailant. Crew members and slaves alike slid and crashed into cargo, each other, oar handles.

An ocean giant picked up the boat and slammed it into the sea. Men flailed as they soared. Some returned; others disappeared into the dark waters. There was shouting as men tied themselves to cargo, the oar holes, and whatever they could reach. The giant picked up the boat and thrashed it into the sea again. Cargo broke free, and ropes snapped. Goods and men flung into the sea. The hand of the raging seas caused Jesus to shoot across the deck into the ocean. Beside him was a man clinging to a floating box. Jesus desperately clung to the box and tried to breathe. There was a gurgle as the box released its last breath and sank. Jesus felt the rope about him being pulled. He knew he was being pulled toward a watery grave. He frantically clung to a man who raged against the ocean where the box had been.

As the crew worked to pull Jesus onto the ship, they found he was not alone. The seas were starting to settle now. The rain beat their bodies as they tied the sail from edge to edge of the ship. Now out of reach of the sky's anger, everyone lay exhausted.

It took an eternity before everybody began to stir. The crew counted, rearranged, and secured the cargo, the captain staring at the sky above the setting sun, and The Voice and Jesus dragging the anchor to the boat's edge and letting it plunge into the depth. The boat swirled between two earth giants while beneath the setting sun.

The man Jesus had clung to approached with a piece of bread. He ripped the bread in half and handed half to Jesus. Jesus reached out a hand with the bread toward The Voice. The man stopped him. He pointed at the bread and then back at Jesus, "Eat." Then walked away to rejoin the crew around the flickering torch that now glowed at the end of the ship.

"Here, take this quickly and eat," Jesus said as he handed The Voice a piece of the bread.

"Why did you save that man? We are slaves. It is not our duty to save the lives of those who abuse us."

"I didn't mean to. I was scared to die. God is mad at me. I failed my father; my brother is gone."

"Find your honor in all things. Even in slavery, we bring honor to our families because there is no god here. Death is our companion. We can only dream of marrying it soon. When I am finally permitted to die, I will return as an ocean bird so I can always fly and be free of men."

"We are not birds. Men do not fly like birds or angels," Jesus said incredulously. "If you are an angel or bird, spread your wings and fly us away from this place."

The man reproached them and interned them into their minuscule dungeon.

"Listen to me. There once was a man who lived on a hill. He was bloodthirsty and killed everything he could find. One day, a serpent spoke to him and told him that if he continued in his ways, he would be reborn as a tortoise who would be the pet of a mighty emperor. He did not listen. Not long after, he was slain by the combined armies of several enemies. I say to you, he was reborn as a tortoise. The fiercest tortoise ever to walk the earth. One day, the tortoise was walking the beach and came across the sleeping man in his path. With his blood-thirsty spirit, he bit the toe off of that man. That man was the new emperor. Instead of the emperor having the tortoise killed, he caged it. The emperor seared the skin of that tortoise every day with a hot iron. His children felt great delight when they were allowed to do the same. It is said that the tortoise lived for over 150 years. What we do in this life decides what happens in our next life."

"My religion has no such beliefs. We are not our gods. We are the children of God."

"Maybe it is God who decides who his children are reborn. My parable is about making sure you are the best you can be in this life to be rewarded in the next."

Jesus was too tired to respond and instead focused on whispering his prayers to God, asking for strength, wisdom, and guidance. Jesus no longer knew if he was dreaming, awake, or somewhere in between.

The next time the boat was still, Jesus emerged and was startled by the blanket of green covering the lands as far as he could see through the fog. The crew instructed Jesus and The Voice to sit in the blood-stained spot on the deck.

After two days of waiting, three other ships approached. They were assembled with the same black wood in the same shape. Men from the boat started shouting, "Hail us, we approach. Have you glory?"

"The crew on Jesus's ship returning, "We have all the glory! Shall you join us?"

"We will share in the glory and claim it for ourselves."

"We shall see, brothers! Bring the horses so we may be on our way!"

The crew began moving from ship to shore. Only Ulrich and Vahnsel remain aboard.

"Slaves," spoke Ulrich, "we shall wait to see if there is any glory here. The witches and warlocks who roam these lands have deep magic. They are ghosts who disappear into the mist and reappear with the sharpest dagger seen by mortals. I hunger to meet my ghosts again," Ulrich exposed his thigh to reveal a jagged pink scar, "I owe them a kiss. Not even the demons found here can keep us from the copper and gold they protect. Have you slaves been face to face with a demon?"

In unison, "never" as Vahnsel turned to Ulrich and held a flat hand in the air.

"Now might be your chance. Quiet now. Go and hide behind that cargo. Demons approach," Ulrich whispered. Jesus could only see green smothered by the grey but quietly crouched and hid behind the cargo.

Ulrich and Vahnsel lowered their frames close to the deck as they crouched away from each other into the mist. A single ripple could be heard in the water. Jesus crouched into a tiny ball, hands and legs trembling, forgetting to breathe.

A clay-white form stepped and pulled itself on the boat, then another, then two more. They whispered among themselves while crouching low. Two of the men started crawling toward where Ulrich and Vahnsel had vanished. The other two slowly crawled towards Jesus. Jesus pushed The Voice back and contorted it between two containers. Jesus crouched and began to pray in a low, deep whisper.

Suddenly, there was a hiss in Jesus's ear. Women demons of pure white, whiter than any sand or clay or cloud, crouched naked beside Jesus. The demon closest to Jesus raised an orange blade high into the air. Jesus's leg shot forth uncontrollably and struck the demon in her right breast. The demon was thrown back as she grabbed her unclad breast.

The second demon leaped into the air at Jesus as he fearfully pressed close his eyes.

A warm mist sprayed across Jesus's face. As his eyes slowly opened, the demon's face stared at him as it rolled off its stem and dully landed at his feet, still blinking. The body was being pushed over the side by Vahnsel. Ulrich dispatched the other demon a few steps past Vahnsel.

"Well, you slaves faced your first demons and weren't dispatched to the underworld. It seems the gods may have plans for you after all," Ulrich laughed. "Come, take these heads and cast them into the sea. This ship has no room for the spirits of demons. They can bring themselves back to life. We shall be gone long before that." Ulrich then turned his attention to the sky, "Have you glory or death, brothers?"

"Glory to us," returned several voices from the void.

"Take this bucket and rinse this demon's blood from the ship. Demon blood is a bad omen we cannot risk."

As the water from the buckets finally began to fade into pink, then clear trotting could be heard. It grew louder, closer, and more crowded. Faint figures darkened into distant silhouettes, and then men on horses began to emerge. The horses carrying burgeoning sacks sank their hooves deep into the green, flinging brown into the sky with each step.

"Have you glory brothers?" Boomed Ulrich.

"Much glory for us and you," replied the captain of Jesus's ship. "Prepare to board our steads."

As the horses were dragged up the ramp, trotted across the deck, and stabled between stacked cargo, Jesus heard the captain speaking to Ulrich and Vahnsel. "Juronig is in mixed glory. Watch yourself and your family when we are home. He has lost two horses and three crew. It seems the gods have found no favor in him. He blames our venture and has a sharp sword. If you join any of his ventures, the gods may send you to the underworld."

"Slave, come here," firmly spoke Troit. "Do you know how to read?" Jesus indicated he did. "Take this slave and learn it. You are not of us. Learn of your gods and your ways." Troit handed Jesus a bag containing a full Tenakh. "You will keep this in that storage container until we reach Vulverno. You saved my life. My debt is paid. That is the way of our gods."

Jesus and The Voice had spent many days gently rocking to and fro. Now, the waves seemed larger and colder. They both were covered from foot to face with tiny bumps that caused them to tremble uncontrollably. Their lips were purple and chapped as they finally emerged from the hole. The crew all stared at them and broke into hysterically laughing.

"Get the slaves some skins," ordered the captain. "They aren't any good to us frozen."

"Here, wear these," Ulrich gave the men boots, pants, and an upper body skin. It took several hours for the shaking to stop while the bow continued dipping into ocean mist. They were thankful the skins protected them from the worst of it.

"Slaves come and sit," ordered the captain. "I know you can understand me, will you speak? Let me hear your words." The group spoke for several hours, the captain telling them many of the rules, the people, and the land of Vulverno. "The gods will test you. You may be dispatched from this world in short order unless you listen. Listen fully if you wish to be dispatched with honor and wealth." The captain spoke with them for several hours, "Now, return to your sleeping place."

It had been several days since the captain spoke to them. They began to wonder and talk about how long it would take to reach Vulverno. It was such a foreign, cold, hostile land. The suffocating grey mist and green fields were almost a distant memory. It had been weeks since they saw land. The horses joined their restlessness, braying and stamping their hooves.

Jesus opened his eyes when he heard yelling. The ship was calm; the crew was not. The horses clopped across the deck above. A hand holding a cup in the sun beaming through the hole. Jesus's eyes were accustomed to the changes in light now, his eyes drawing into focus seconds after he was birthed from the hole from the last time.

"Come boys," ordered Ulrich in a cheery, almost pleasant call. "You shall unload the goods one last time. The gods will decide your fate this day. Jesus and The Voice unloaded all of the cargo into eight stacks. Boxes, sacks, and debris lined the dock. Jesus and The Voice started walking back to the boat. "Where are you two going? Your sea voyage is over. You stand here, you stand down there."

Men, women, and children sang, drank, and embraced in great numbers. Some families only found sorrow. The captain handed a small sack of coins to each family who had lost someone. Troit walked to Jesus with three young men and a hearty woman. "Slave, grab a box. You will serve my family. These are your new masters," Troit waved an arm at the young men and the woman. "Boys, here's our servant. Any damage which befalls him will be removed from your wealth and honor."

"What is his name?"

"His name is Slave. Now grab those sacks and off with us. I have traveled too far. Your mother needs my private attention to recover from my absence."

CHAPTER III

The House of Troit
Kailum

"That is Thor, the protector of gods and man who has slain many jötnar. That is Sif. That is Odin and Frigg, the pursuer of knowledge and the knowledge of the future. That is Baldr, the son of Odin and Frigg, who resides in Hel," Jesus was finishing the recital, demonstrating his knowledge of the small statues on the mantle.

"The god of the Jews created man from dirt and then a woman from the man's ribs. He is a jealous and angry god that demands unfettered obedience and loyalty. He sounds like a few of the men and gods who walk around these lands," Troit volleyed his knowledge of Jesus's god back.

"My god is not of men. He is a fair and just god. He has chosen my people to multiply and spread throughout the world. He," Troit raised his hand.

"Your god may have selected you to travel throughout the world, yet you are a slave. You serve me, your bother was cleaved to bits while you watched, and you have no wife or children. You do not multiply. Where is your god? It seems he has the same temperament as Loki. Maybe they are long-lost friends. Finish memorizing the Tenakh. It is the way of your people. You must know it, memorize it. You are not of us. You will not be favored by our gods nor our ways."

"Father, speaking of Loki," Gönig was removing his mud-covered boots as he entered. "Juronig is restless and filled with drink again. He is going on about how you owe him for his failures. We must prepare for his visit."

"No, Loki has a mind for us to clash. We know what happened when Hŭlœg tired of Loki's games and faced Juronig. I do not intend my family to see such a fate. Come, Odin will guide us where we may collect a stag for a feast. Jesus, prepare the horses."

"Father," whispered Gönig as Jesus softly closed the door behind him, "why must you call him by name? It brings dishonor to our family."

"Son, you know he has earned the right. Odin has given him favor with the gift of knowledge for a slave. Thor has given him great strength for a slave."

"If you will not protect our name, then I must. I will not travel with you to gather the feast. Watch for the elves. They are at play this time of year."

"Be gone with you. I have sent many an elf to the underworld. Go and fetch your brother. Tomorrow evening, we feast."

As Jesus and Troit dismounted at the large pine by the broadleaf weed-filled clearing, Troit whispered, "You have brought great honor and wealth despite Loki's tricks. Odin has truly blessed you with knowledge. So I shall impart more to you in praise of Odin. See the Stag?" Troit silently pointed, and Jesus winked in response. "Aim, if you claim success, I will show you how we honor the gods with the sacrifice of this beast."

Jesus jostled when he drew the arrow taut. The arrow flip-flopped through the air and flew far above the target. "Hahahaha, you have the skills of a mist ghost. Surely, Loki enjoys playing with your fate. Keep practicing. You will have the skills I learned from the Scotts soon enough. Have I taught you how to speak Scotts yet? No? We shall work on that. They are the only ghosts that strike fear into many of the men here. Knowing their language may bring wealth in trade or spare your soul if Loki keeps his temperament. Come, we shall go fishing."

The braided reed basket was nearly filled as the sun finally peaked in the sky. Fish hopelessly flopped against the deep sides as Jesus pulled the basket to a low, flat rock. The head and tail were removed quickly. Fingering through the meat to pick the bones away took an extended time.

"What are you doing there, Jesus? Stop that. Why are you mutilating that fish and wasting so much? Grab the fish by the gills and rip out its mouth and innards like this. Lay it down on its side and stretch it out. Enter the knife right at the gill and slice it in two longways. Remove the bones in one clean pull and then slice the tail bits. You see, this way, I have four pieces of fish, each the size of one of yours. Feed four men instead of one by using the whole of the fish. Now pass me that wine."

"The wineskins are dry. I am afraid I have not prepared enough wine for our day."

"I have had that wineskin for a great number of harvests. Pass it to me. I shall show you one more thing this day. You must not reveal this as it is our magic."

The fear in Jesus's heart towards magic was only surpassed by his fear of Troit. Naturally, his hand trembled as he held out the wineskin. "I think I have had a bit of wine. You will be the magic man today. Go and fill that skin at the creek. Fill it halfway with water and bring it here. I will start a fire while you go."

When Jesus returned, Troit had several round stones in a small inferno. A large green leaf bowl lay fireside. "Mash the skin well to mix the water. Shake it. Good, now come pour that water in this bowl." Troit used a stick and his sword to move each rock from the blaze and plop them in the water. A great fury of steam and boil rose from the liquid. "See how it rages? That is what we want. The angrier the water, the better this will work. We must always ensure the skins are old. Much wine has been stored within and dried into the skins. We shall reclaim it. Come, be careful, and pour this water back into the skin. Slosh, mush, and shake. Good, now go. Dip the skin in the stream to cool it."

As Jesus poured the pink liquid into the two wooden travel cups, Troit smiled, "See there, you have learned my magic. Taste it and tell me if it is wine or water."

Jesus sipped the cup, "This surely is god's magic."

"No, just a simple trick. We just reclaimed the wine from the skin. Look in there. Is the inside of the skin still stained with the years of wine?"

"No, it is like new."

"Yes, we have no magic. We have just cleaned the wine that was always there. Now, guide my horse. I had a lot of wine and meat. I have grown tired. Take me to Depillr to see the eel."

The sun was on its way to retreating from the moon as they approached the hidden pond. Troit had returned to his senses as Jesus rode behind. A faint murmuring could be heard.

Troit turned and motioned Jesus to take the horses as he silently dismounted and disappeared into the woods. "By the heavens, Jesus, come now."

From the base of a small hill, Jesus's eyes transfixed on the site and froze.

"Jesus, have you ever seen such dishonor as this?"

"I have seen that many times, but it has been many years."

"In the lands of your god?"

"Yes, those who have committed great sins against man are punished in such a way."

"You there, have you committed great sins against man?"

A naked, bloody figure gasped, "I have done nothing. Please, please, end me now. I wish to join the great spirit warriors who live with Father Sky and Mother Earth."

"If you have done nothing, why do you find yourself on this wood? My people would have performed the blóðœrn. I see no wings upon your back. Who has done these things to you?"

"Please, I am a great warrior from across the great river. Finish me with honor."

"You do not wish to be saved?"

"No, I wish to rejoin my people in the sky and woods. I am a healer and a warrior, not a witch."

"Then I shall cut you down, then you shall serve me from this day forward. I have no fear of witches. You are far too tiny a man to be a great warrior. Jesus, tip this wood and help me remove these stakes."

The blood pulsating from the unknown soul soaked the slippery stakes. Moving to the man's feet, Jesus slipped and impaled his leg on a jagged spike that splintered from the beam. It took Jesus and Troit several hours to remove and bandage the man.

"Jesus, bandage yourself, man. You may be worse off than our new claim."

"There, on the ground. Bring me that sinew. I will mend you."

Troit removed his sword and placed it on the man's chest. "Do as he asks Jesus," turning his attention to the man, "Don't tempt your fate, witch. You may be a great warrior and healer, but I am skilled at causing great pain without death."

Jesus handed the man the dried tendon. The man picked up a sharp sliver, "This will cause displeasure, but it will keep the mischievous spirits from entering your body." He quickly penetrated Jesus's flesh beside the wound and worked the tendon through. He continued crisscrossing the tendon the length of the wound and pulled it hard. "There now, when this is healed, cut the sinew here and pull it out. The bleeding has stopped, yet the healing has just begun."

"Jesus, look at that magic. He has saved you. Now, you must ensure his life is saved. I shall forfeit yours if you fail. All men have value, so we only kill those who do not bring us fortune. This witch has great magic we can use to build our fortunes."

"Surely God left this man here to suffer. This punishment is not from your people. It is from the followers of my god."

"Perhaps your god left this man here to teach you about power and wealth. This man has no power. Now I use him to build my wealth," Troit snarled in a way that reminded Jesus, 'a slave with privileges was still a slave.' "Remember, if he dies, you will join him on his journey to the underworld. Put him on your horse. We will make for the safer grounds."

The silence of the rising sun was met with the shattering as milk flowed across the floor.

"Jesus! Why hasn't our great warrior learned to carry a simple milk jug? It has been two whole days. From this moment, all his sins will be paid with your blood. Now, go and fetch my good whip."

"Surely I cannot be held responsible for such a slave," Jesus frantically rebutted while he dragged the injured foot as he entered the room. His wound had swelled, dripped with puss, and caused near lameness.

"You forget your place, Jesus," turning to the new slave, "Great warrior, come here. Jesus is not above a fellow slave. For his insolence, he shall ensure your wounds are kept clean. You have no value if he cannot walk. Jesus, wash his feet. This will be your new responsibility to remind you how you are a servant placed above no others."

"I will do as you ordered and bring honor and glory to your family," Jesus managed to force the words through the agony burning his leg.

As Jesus and the man made their way to the cow pasture, the man spoke softly, "I can heal myself. You are too injured to help anyone. Let me, instead, heal you. There are many plants here that have great healing properties. If you grind that one into a powder and then drink it, all forms of cough dissipate. That round one over there will remove soreness in the knees, and that one can be chewed and placed into a wound to prevent rot and soothe," he grabbed a bunch and began chewing. "That one will cause a man to stop breathing in moments while that spine-covered one will prevent ocean madness." The man continued that way for quite some time as they milked.

"Why do you offer to help me? I was going to let you suffer on the cross," the offer confounded Jesus.

"How's your leg doing? It looks quite red and oozes. Give it here." The man grabbed his leg and then spat the wad of the plant onto his stitched wound before Jesus had a chance to respond. Pressing it into the wound with a thumb, the man pushed Jesus's chest back with the other to defeat all resistance. Jesus clenched his jaw tightly and swallowed his scream to prevent Troit from hearing the commotion and following through with his promise of a whipping.

The man stepped back and helped Jesus to his feet a moment later. "Walk there and then back here and see if that helps."

The pain had dissipated from Jesus's leg. Now, it felt renewed and strengthened. "Teach me your magic witch."

"I am not a which I am of the people of the shining river, the Wolastoqiyik."

CHAPTER IV

Changing Tides

"Father, Juronig has won the council's favor," Gönig said as he entered. The flicker of the candle danced the shadows about the room. "We must prepare our houses. I am sure there will be support from old friends."

"No, it seems Loki has finally won the day. We cannot fight a god. When Odin and Thor return, they will take care of Loki, and then we shall swiftly dispatch Juronig."

"Shall I secure the slaves then, or will you bring them to the celebration?"

Jesus overheard the conversation and retreated to the slave quarters. Haling Dog was resting from a long day of lumber harvesting.

"Gönig has arrived. He is saying Juronig has taken the council. I have heard many conversations about Juronig. He is a fundamental theist. He spreads the gospel of northern purity, superiority, and isolation. If he has truly taken over the council, we are in grave danger," Jesus whispered.

"Shall we fight, or shall we run?" Healing dog whispered back. "Are the swords and bow still by the kiln?"

"Troit will not be easy to slay. He is a very cunning and fierce warrior. I have seen many true northern beasts of men, bear and wolf, slain using his bare hands," Jesus finished whispering as Troit and Gönig stepped into the room.

"What are you two speaking about?" Troit asked, staring at Jesus. Troit sliced an apple and then used the knife to eat the slice as he stared.

"We were talking about the day's labors," Jesus's voice quivered as he looked at the floor.

"Look at me while we speak!" Troit's voice boomed in the small room. "I know you listened as my son gave me the news."

"Yes, I heard, but not on purpose."

"You know what this means. Does your friend know how things will be changed?" Troit motioned towards Healing Dog.

"You will sacrifice us to Loki," Jesus's voice trailed to silence.

"No, we are not sons of Loki. We are sons of Odin and Thor. We will honor them. There is a cave in the woods. You will live there until Odin returns. We have provided you with the knowledge you require to survive."

"If they are found?" Gönig interjected.

"If they are found, they will be tortured in the most painful of ways. Our fate will surely follow soon after."

"Let us pray Odin returns shortly," Gönig was nearly inaudible.

"If you are discovered," Troit turned back to Jesus and Healing Dog, "You will say you escaped us. We will do what we can in these times. If you are captured, all may prove futile. You have secured for us great wealth and respect. You have saved my and Gönig's lives plenty to de- serve a fighting chance. We repay you in this way and return to you some sliver of the honor you have bestowed on our families."

"We are greatly honored. We will survive and thus continue to bring honor to your families," Jesus knew the risks the men were taking to let them live and was overwhelmed with gratitude and relief.

"We leave now. Leave your things. You are escaped slaves who did not have time to pack. We have collected a bag of food and a dagger. You have also stolen a sword each."

"We can never repay this debt," Jesus began to speak.

"Stop," Gönig interrupted, "repay us by not getting caught. Surely, if you get caught, the torture of our families will be far greater than a brain such as yours can imagine."

As they descended into the cave, all wind, noise, and light vanished. Jesus's senses were completely blinded. He jumped backward, smashing his elbow against a damp, flat rock. His scream echoed into eternity.

"Quiet down there," Gönig whispered, but the command was stern. Healing Dog Clasped one hand over Jesus's mouth and another on the back of his head.

"I am lowering firewood. An ember sits atop. Move it away from the ropes but not under the rocks. You both have what you need. I must return before it is discovered I am gone. Stay alive and stay hidden until I or my father return. Come out for no others." With that, the sound of Gönig's trot receded into the woods.

The food bag had lasted several days before Jesus and Healing Dog grew restless. They craved meat.

"Come, Jesus, let me teach you how my people make a bow. We need the meat. The swords are useless against deer and rabbits."

"Teach me all of your ways. Someday, the things I learn may save me or the lives of those who can bring me a fortune."

"A bow can surely save you and bring you a fortune. The spirits may provide gifts of meat. If they do, we need the skill to honor them and accept the gifts."

"The only spirits who live here are the gods of the northerners, my companion. Let us climb from the pit where we reside so we may hunt."

Jesus's elbow was still raw and caused his arm to shake as he released an arrow. The stag lept into the air as the arrow found its mark. As it landed, it somersaulted as its front legs collapsed.

"No, too organized. You must scatter the leaves more," Jesus whispered as he dragged the deer. "If they are in a line like that, it makes a trail. We use the leaves to hide our retreat, not expose it."

Healing Dog began scattering the leaves wider. The strokes of his foot extended beyond the lines made by the dragged carcass. "Snap!"

Healing Dog fell to the ground, clasping his leg. He bit his lip. Although muffled, his squeal still permeated the foliage.

"What has happened," Jesus ran and covered Healing Dog's mouth. "Let me see," Jesus brushed the leaves away from Healing Dog's boot.

"Careful," Healing Dog's face was still red with agony. "Remove my boot and see it has finally killed me."

"If what has killed you? What is wrong with your foot?" Jesus asked as he delicately unlashed and removed the boot.

A tan-creamy puss with slivers of bright red oozed from Healing Dog's big red swollen toe. It felt hot on Jesus's hand. The touch caused Healing Dog to wince in pain.

"This is bad. How long has your foot been like this?" Jesus asked as he drew the dagger. "I have seen this before. The nail has grown into the skin. We need to remove it and drain the puss."

"How do you know these things?"

"Troit removed mine. Mine was never this bad. We may need to take the whole toe. All this sickness spilling forth is severe." Jesus placed the edge of the dagger against the toenail.

"Not here. I cannot contain my pain. Someone will hear. The pain subsides. Let's get our meet back to the cave. We will make a bit of leather into a bit to help me bite through the pain."

"Let us make our way then," Jesus replied, "but you must leave the boot off. Scatter the leaves the best you can; be quick."

The dagger rested in the fire beside a thick strip of skin. Meat seared on sticks above.

"The dagger and bit are ready. Roll this skin and put it in your mouth. It will keep you from biting off your tongue before you faint. Make sure your pile of leaves and moss catches you," Jesus handed the skin to Healing Dog. The flesh of a different buck skin hissed as Jesus used it to lift the dagger. He poured water on Healing Dog's puss-drenched toe and wiped it with a green leaf.

"Bite now," Jesus empathetically commanded in a soft tone. He was sliding the dagger's edge down the center of Healing Dog's toenail.

Healing Dog's clenched jaw gargled, face burned red, and veines erupted from his face and neck momentarily before he slumped backward. Jesus tossed the dagger into the rocks on the far edge of the cave. He clenched Healing Dog's foot and ripped the infected nail upward with the force of ten men. As a thick section of the nail was freed from the tomb of blood and puss, the end remained attached by the cuticle. Jesus dashed to retrieve the dagger and sever the finalize the operation. Afterward, Jesus removed the leather bit from Healing Dog's mouth, wrapped the toe with herbs, and feasted on freshly cooked meat.

"I will rewash your feet. I will check to see if we are healed," Jesus said as they ate berries while traveling to gather more water.

"It has returned to good order. How long do you think we should live in this place," Healing Dog tried to change the subject.

"It will not be much longer before we are returned to the house of Troit. I will still be checking your feet often. The loss of one foot could result in losing both of our lives."

"So, maybe two more full moons?"

"Have patience. Troit will return and see how we have honored him. We will return to the family and serve with honor again soon."

"We can run away. Will you go with me?"

"There is nothing beyond this place for either of us. We will not run. We are not cowards. We have honor. Plus, where would we go? No matter where we go, we will be murdered if seen."

"We can go to my home," Healing Dog suggested. "My people will reward you with great honor, riches, and a family."

"Why does your honor fade?" Questioned Jesus.

"It is my honor that fades?" Healing Dog scoffed, "No, my honor doesn't fade, my friend. I can see the omens. The spirits speak to me as well. Darkness is coming."

"Sit, we have reached the water. Let me see if your omens and honor have made you lose your toe." Healing Dog's toe had scarred into a pink mound of gnarled toenail and puffy skin. "Your spirits have permitted you to survive once more."

As Jesus gazed at the stars through the treetops from the cave, he heard footsteps. He doused the fire as he shook Healing Dog's leg. Cementing Healing Dog's mouth closed with a firm grip, Jesus whispered, "Someone approaches."

They both clung tightly to the side of the cave, trying to sink from sight. The footsteps had reached the top of the cave wall and stopped. The rope beside Jesus shook and then stopped. It shook once more. Jesus slowly drew the dagger as he spotted the swords on the rocks across the cave.

"Slaves, are you down there?" A voice whispered. It was unfamiliar. The men remained motionless. A torch suddenly appeared on the ground so closely the heat warmed Jesus's legs.

The command grew slightly louder, "Slaves, come now. We must free you from this. . . " The articulation trailed off. A body then appeared on the burning torch, thick red streams flowing from the thin bits of flesh that still connected the head to the shoulders.

"Jesus, Healing Dog, you have been discovered," the sound of Troit was aged and raspy. "Come now and be freed. I have a ship to take you from this place."

As the sun rose, the men finally could see Troit. His eyes were sunken, his belly shrunken, and many wrinkles draped his face. They walked in silence for hours until they heard the soothing sounds of the sea.

Troit was the first to speak, "They killed my son. He hung in the village, flesh burned, as birds feasted on him. I will not be voyaging with you. The ship is there, beyond that mound. It isn't much. Yet, it will get you to the land of Scotts. My people will not find you there."

"We will return with you and avenge your family," Jesus retorted. "We are not so weak that we must dishonor you or run from those who dishonor your family."

"Do you think me needing to use the hand of slaves for vengeance will bring honor? No, you will go. You will survive. You are freed to ensure at least one loss for my enemies. They will not have the pleasure of your blood."

"If you go alone. . ."

"I know what fate Loki has designed for me upon my return. I die with honor as is our way. Now go and make your way. You are free. Go, return to your ways and escape the clutches of Loki."

CHAPTER V

Chasing Eternity

Jesus and Healing-Dog catapulted forward as the frail makeshift ship slid to an abrupt halt. Miraculously, they had somehow evaded the northerner's patrols, the tumultuous frozen waves, to reach the land of the Scotts. They would live to see at least one more day if they could enter the woods.

"The spirits will continue to protect and guide us. Have faith," Healing-Dog reassured as he helped Jesus to his feet.

"Troit placed himself in grave danger by refusing to execute us. The new council of the Northerns will surely put him to death if we are reached. We must not stay in the land of the Scotts any longer than needed," Jesus was brushing sand from his arms and chest.

"Then let's make our way before the Scotts arrive."

It had been several days since they completed their tiny mud cave in the roots of a tree on the side of the forest hill. The crisp air crackled as the low flames licked the rabbit. "Crack," the woods whispered.

"I am going to take a walk and make room for our feast," whispered Healing-Dog as he slowly and silently picked up his bow and quiver.

Jesus nodded, "I shall go and fetch us some more water from the stream." He carefully placed the skin bladder harness over his shoulder and stood. They both pointed in opposite directions and walked into the woods.

Jesus slowly placed each foot softly on the naked ground. He ensured no twig, leaf, or branch betrayed his approach. As Jesus neared his earthen home, he could see a shadowy figure pulling the rabbit from its firey roost. The figure picked it up, "Ouch," then dropped it.

Jesus ran into the clearing, "Quiver your arrow, Healing Dog!"

The half-naked, emaciated figure ran into the woods. With each step, the skin about his ribs constricted enough to see his beating heart.

"Jesus, why did you stop me from dispatching the Scottish thief?"

"That was no Scott. That was a voice I had not seen in many years. We shall feed him so we may be reborn as hawks."

"A spirit hawk is one of the most powerful. Yes, let us seek such a noble destiny. The ground here is soft. This may be a short journey if his stamina meets his ribs."

The forest progressed from dark to black as the men agreed to continue in the morning. They gathered fresh greens from the surrounding flora and made a bed. They were unaware of the surrounding life; thus, any desire for an evening fire or warmth dissipated with the setting sun. The evening winds subsided as they heard a "clunk," then another, and another. The clunking found the men using melodic reverberations.

"Jesus, surely we know that sound. The sun shall rise soon. Let's make our way to the noise. We shall see if pillagers make their way in this direction."

"Yes, and if god is smiling upon us, maybe they have left their cargo without a guard. We can alleviate them of some of their responsibility."

It was hard to believe a single tiny sea vessel bobbed in the minuscule lagoon. It was sealed from the ocean by a low, narrow strip of sand.

"They must have abandoned it when they ran aground. There will be nothing we can use. Surely, they have claimed all they could."

"Have faith, Healing Dog. The craft itself is our loot," Jesus whispered into the wind.

"Unless the spirits fly this vessel on their wings, it will remain here, useless to us."

"Healing Dog, the spirits will not be the ones to free this great ship. Surely, you have moved lands before. Do you remember flattening the hill for Troit's farm?"

"This is sand, not rock, mud, and root."

"Come, let us see if anybody is home."

Even though the water only rose to their chests, getting aboard was quite a struggle with neither hook nor ladder. They collapse as Jesus finally flopped Healing-Dog onto the Deck, unable to catch their breaths from their exertions.

"Surely, nobody is here. We can see the entire ship."

"It's perfect, Healing Dog. Now, let us check to see if it floats. Pull that latch. If the water beneath us is more than a forearm deep, the ship cannot float. I lived in such a place when I first left my father's house."

The door was stuck. Jesus joined Healing-Dog as they pulled the rope latch, their entire bodies springing upright and abruptly being stopped by the cord.

"Keep pulling. It is starting to give. Here, look, a small edge has appeared. Pull! Pull!" As the door thrashed open, the men thought a murmur was heard.

"Are you a ghost or a man in there? Come out so I may dispatch you from this place, demon," commanded Jesus.

"Which master do you serve?" The speech was familiar to Jesus.

"I serve no master. We were released to this life because we were so good in the last."

"I, too, have been released from my last life so I may not perish at the hand of the evil. How do I know you are not tricking me?"

"Come, see for yourself. The northern masters freed us so they would not have to dispatch us to the next life."

The frame no longer had the lean muscle Jesus had remembered. The man looked like a hollow skeleton of a former self. "Take this. Share this feast as we once did so long ago." Jesus removed from his pouch a small piece of jerked rabbit. Tearing it in half, he gave a piece to The Voice.

"We do not have enough to share," Healing-Dog objected.

"He will eat from my rations then. Like you, he is a great healer and spiritual guide. He serves our needs far better alive unless you mean to eat him. There is not much on the bone for the picking. Do you want to have such a meager meal?"

"Even the most ferrel of forest spirits would not eat such a man."

"It is settled then. Join us in our last supper as prisoners of this island, or choose to remain here with the Scotts."

As the men wrestled the boat through the shallow trench, the ocean soaked their lower while sweat soaked their chest and brow. As the front of the craft began to bob with the surf, the men walked to the rear and began to push.

"Success, friends. Tie the ropes about you and hold on. When the ship sails, I will pull each of you aboard," Jesus began climbing aboard.

"Do not delay. We shall sail this day," chanted the men. That chant had become a daily prayer. Every day for a month, they had inched the boat across the final pinnacle of sand at high tide. Never before had it bobbed. "Jesus, the surf breaks it free! Pull us aboard! We shall be on our way!"

The sun was high in the sky now, and the tide had left them. The ship continued steadily wobbling on the waves. The day migrated into the evening as the men succumbed to exhaustion.

Jesus felt a shock weave its way from his foot to his hip. Then again, "Jesus, the spirits have pushed us to the ocean. The Scott's land low below father sky as the sun appears."

Jesus lay there as he felt the soothing caress of the ocean beneath. As he stared at Healing Dog, he inquired, "Now what?"

"Now we return to my land, the land of my spirits. There are more woodland creatures and fish than you could eat in one hundred lifetimes. My people will celebrate and honor you for returning their healer."

"Then let us be gone. How will we find our way to this land of plenty?"

"Father Sky will guide us during the day while the hunter will point us towards home at night."

"Where is our friend?"

"He has counted the rations and started fishing for breakfast so that we may keep our jerky until it is needed."

"Let us join him. There are no servants in this place."

"The storm took all but a day's worth of greens. The hunter has fled south. We must turn south to follow his lead. We only have enough water left for two more days if we drink half of our need," The Voice informed.

Healing Dog began to sing and stamp his feet. He raised his arms to the sky and whooped to the clouds.

Jesus stepped forward to interrupt as a white bird descended through the clouds, dove into the ocean and then took flight.

Healing Dog turned to his companions, "Come, the spirits have sent us a guide. Let us follow so we may be saved."

Shortly after, they could see a giant white mountain rising from the horizon. Then, a black line topped with green appeared below. As they neared, large rocks jutted from the white-fleck-covered beach.

"Those are not patches of snow. We must prepare to defend ourselves as we claim this land. Do not take any eggs. Just move swiftly beyond the beach. We shall find what this place has to offer before they soar."

"Healing Dog, why do your spirits attack us?" Yelled The Voice through the thick screeches. "We are not even within an arrow's flight from the beach."

"They are warning us from this place. Surely, we should turn and sail to a safer spot!"

They quickly reached a consensus while trying to bat their airborne assailants with their swords.

Within an hour, they had passed the mountain and found the mouth of a small stream that wound its way through the black sand.

As they made their way up the stream, the sand faded into rock, then fields.

"Come, Healing Dog, collect herbs with me so we may make elixers, lotions, and medicines," The Voice suggested.

Healing Dog stuffed a handful of dandelions in his mouth, "let's fatten our bellies as we do it. Jesus, refill the water containers so we can prepare to leave quickly." With a wave of the arm, Jesus started working his way to the ship.

The sun was getting low in the sky when Jesus started floating the last barrel of water to the ship. The tides had receded. Getting the barrel off the beach caused Jesus's legs to burn with exhaustion. His arms quivered with fatigue. His eyes burned so intensely with sweat that he failed to realize the ship no longer rocked with the waves.

"Jesus, come and join us," shouted a voice from a low fire just beyond the black sands.

"Here, drink," The Voice handed Jesus a cup that contained white flower petals, purple flower petals, small purple berries, and steaming water. "Careful, it's hot. We have been trying these plants all day. They have given us renewed life."

"And sit on this carpet. It protects from the rocks," Healing Dog waved a hand across a large blanket of soft moss. "We can sleep like kings this evening. Place more wood on the fire and let us enjoy being alive, free, and having food and drink."

Jesus, too tired to respond, sat silently and watched the fire dance. As he drank, he could feel the warm fluid slowly flow down his throat, warm his belly, and spread throughout his limbs. His exhaustion became overwhelming as he lay back on the moss and stared at the stars. The other two men had made make-shift walls with skins and wood shafts.

"Come, let me check your feet. You have journeyed far in the past days," Jesus instructed the men to sit beside the stream. As he washed their feet, he painstakingly checked for any signs of damage, rot, ingrown nails, or blisters. "You have a blister here, between these toes.

Use this leaf by chewing it and wrapping it on the blister for two days." The men then returned to the ship to find they could not depart the island. They enjoyed the fresh fruit and hot potions over the next few days.

A small ice obelisk rose from the ocean ahead only a day after their previous refuge had vanished. As the tower raised, its base widened as far as the men could see.

"We are nearly home. The spirits have guided us true," Healing Dog was manic, screaming, pointing, and laughing.

"Has he lost himself?" The Voice was confounded with a hand on his sword.

"Friend," called out Jesus. "I see no great nation. Not even a village. You have told us great stories about your home. Where is the great nation you have described?"

"Have faith, my friends. I have not gone mad. This land of ice was where we lost three ships when I was taken all those years ago. We shall sail beyond this island. Within a day, you will be rewarded by my people for your courage."

"We only have enough food for a day. I see no land beyond this one," The Voice whispered. "Surely he has gone mad and means to bring us to our water grave."

"We shall stop and refill our fish barrels and water. Then, we shall continue to have faith and see where this life takes us. If we meet a watery fate in this life, surely we will be rewarded in the next."

"I would rather not depart this world soon. I still have more to make up for from my past life."

"Quiet now, cease your fear. We shall finish what we started," Jesus finished whispering. "Healing Dog, you have waited many years to return to the land of your people. One more day will not hurt. We will stop at the island to fish and refill our water."

"We have plenty of water and fish! Let us sail," Healing Dog now foamed with excitement.

"We both agree," Jesus motioned toward The Voice. "We should be prepared if there is a storm in our future."

"You both agree?" Healing Dog looked at The Voice, who rested a hand on his sheathed sword. "Then we shall fish and enjoy one more night at sea.

As the dense green forest came into view, Healing Dog could no longer contain his excitement. He was yipping, hooting, and jumping on the deck. He called to birds and whistled to the forest. When they were a couple hundred yards from the beach, Healing Dog could no longer contain himself and jumped into the water.

Jesus and The Voice could see him run across the beach and into the forest as they found a small lagoon. They dragged the anchor across the deck as The Voice inquired of himself, "Do you think he is coming back?"

"I don't know," Jesus whispered. "I don't know why we are whispering either. But, he has received a great reward. Let's hope he does not forget who helped him claim it."

The first night on land was filled with a sense of accomplishment despite the cool breeze that prevented sleep. They had found this hidden place and survived the oceans.

"Surely," Jesus thought, "the god of my people has rewarded us for knowing the teachings and honoring the word. But I am in the land of spirits now. I must honor them to make my way unmamed."

On the second day, the men created a wood and mud shelter. They covered it with skins and then leafy branches.

"I found some berries down there. They are quite sweet. Something else has been eating them as well. I found a stinking pile near the bushes. It was bigger than any I have ever seen. There may be giants, beasts, or dragons in this land of dark forests," The Voice updated Jesus.

"I finished cooking the bow. Tomorrow, we shall hunt," Jesus replied.

Jesus felt thick, cold fingers crossed his lips and caused his eyes to spring open. Healing Dog squatted over him and whispered, "Where is The Voice." Jesus shrugged.

A heavy rustling, a growl, and a loud snort crept through the mud wall beside Jesus's ear.

Healing Dog yelled something in a language unknown to Jesus and began banging and kicking the wall. The wall shifted inward. Jesus lept shoulder first into Healing Dog's chest. They landed just beyond the collapsed hut. A massive brown bear the size of nine men was growling and towering in the air.

An arrow penetrated the bear. Blood spurted from its neck onto the men. Every spurt shot blood across their faces and then down their necks. Circular droplets dotted their chests.

The bear stepped backward, caught its balance, and stepped forward again. A second arrow struck. Blood now oozed from the bear's chest. It turned, lowered to four legs, teetered a few yards, and collapsed.

"No!" Yelled Healing Dog as he scrambled to the bear. He began to pray in the strange language. "We did not have to attack this spirit. This is a bad omen. The other spirits will not be with us if we are not thankful for this spirit's sacrifice. Come, we shall claim what we can and prepare the rest for the forest spirits such as wolf, fox, and hawk."

Healing Dog was exacting in his extraction of the bearskin. He laid the fur down on the forest floor. The men quickly removed the meat from the bones and placed it on the skin. The skin was folded. Jesus cut slits in the overlapping edges as the other two wove a branch through the sides. The men placed the branch on their shoulders and began to walk.

"We will take this to my tribe. I have told them to prepare for guests. Bringing such an offering will garner much respect."

CHAPTER VI

Brave New World

The treaty was almost finished. Jesus, Healing Dog, and The Voice had been chosen to represent the Wolastoqiyik in the formation of the communal laws of the territory. They now sat and drank burning juice. It made the colors of the dancers, fires, stars, and each other swirl. Each man's smile drove their cheeks into their ears while they tried to maintain their balance through their uncontrollable laughter.

"We have reached paradise," Jesus cackled. "We will be celebrated for eternity."

"We surely will be rewarded in our next life. We shall be kings," The Voice giggled.

"You may be a king, but not me. I will be a sky spirit, probably a hawk. I will live in the house of Father Sky."

Members of other tribes began to join their merriment. Each spoke about how they would be rewarded. Soon, they began to compare the traditions and history of each tribe. Each warrior spoke, telling stories of how their tribes had overcome a great foe to reach greatness. When Jesus's turn arrived, he took time to think about his history.

"My people do not have the honor of being guided by the spirits. We have a god."

"Only one?" A Pigwacket representative inquired as a Sokoki motioned for his silence.

"Yes, my tribe has only one. A long time ago, my tribe was enslaved by a great tribe. They forced us to build for them. Their kings, or chieftains, forced us to create great buildings for worshiping the sun god, farm the fields, and serve their people in homes."

"You mean the pyramids?" An Androscoggin elder interrupted.

Jesus was dumbfounded with a jaw that hung loose. Everything had gone silent other than the crackle of the fire. The dancers and singers were beginning to sit and listen.

"You know about the pyramids? No, my tribe did not build those. We built smaller buildings."

"The stories of great pyramids have been passed down for many years. I last heard the story when I was a young child. I thought the tribes and pyramids in the stories were myths. Do such buildings exist?" The subdued Androscoggin elder had become chatty.

"They do exist. I have seen them," offered The Voice. "I was brought to them once to find hidden riches."

"You stole from the sun god?"

"No, my master found only thirst. We never returned and prayed for forgiveness for trespassing," The Voice knew his infraction had been received poorly.

The elder turned back to Jesus, "Finish telling of how your tribe overcame their masters." The listeners scooted a little closer to ensure no detail escaped their ears.

"The god of my people spoke to our leader. Our leader was commanded to tell the evil king, the pharaoh, to let our people go. He performed miracles for the king to prove God had sent him to the king. The pharaoh refused to free our people, so our god commanded our leader to return and warn the pharaoh. Our leader warned the pharaoh that if he did not let our people go, there would be many plagues that killed many of the pharaoh's people. The pharaoh laughed and mocked our god and cast out our leader. The plagues came. The pharaoh repeatedly promised to let my tribe go, each time recanting. In the end, the god of my tribe killed the firstborn child in every home of the pharaoh's people. The pharaoh let my people leave. Then, his armies chased my tribe to make them slaves once more. The god of my tribe split the sea in two and let my tribe pass through. As the pharaoh's army tried to pass through the sea, it was drowned as the god of my tribed smashed waves upon their heads."

"Your tribe may not have spirits to guide you, but you have a powerful god. What happened once you crossed the sea? Did your tribe find fertile land and prosper?"

"No, our leader refused to obey our god. My tribe was lost in the desert for over forty harvests."

"Ahh. . . We, too, have spirits that hold a grudge. Moose and Squirrel are like that," the elder pointed into the black night.

"Will you tell me more about the great pyramids from your childhood?" Jesus yearned to sit at the table with his mother and father and didn't know why. He had not felt such a way for many years.

"The elders told us many stories. They once told a story of a warrior who traveled the sea searching for the sun god. He took a boat and traveled down the shore for many weeks. He traveled past an island hook, past many great rivers, around lands infested with great green beasts with a long beak of teeth. . ."

Jesus interrupted, knowing it was disrespectful, "I apologize, great and wise leader. Do you mean a Crocodile? Did the beast have short legs with sharp talons?"

"What you describe sounds like the beasts in the stories. They live where the trees grow in water. The warrior traveled the coast down around a long stretch of sand that went on for many days and was covered with these beasts. The story says the sand turned like this," the elder made a 'U" shape in the dirt. "The warrior kept traveling because he had not reached the land of the sun. Yet, the waters were much warmer after the turn. The warrior knew he was approaching the land of the sun. The warrior then passed an immense river of mud. Several days later, the warrior found the land of the sun. The trees had spines like porcupines, not leaves. The grass was dried and dead. No animals could be found. The sun was so angry that his home had been invaded that he made the warrior fall into a deep sleep. When he woke, he was in a strange land where the trees towered and kissed Father Sky. The birds were made of many bright colors. There were people there that captured the warrior. They brought him to their village, where they had lined the streets with decapitated heads on sticks. They enslaved him and forced him to learn the language. He lived in a place with stone buildings and great pyramids. When Father Sky found the warrior had been enslaved, Father Sky grew angry and sent a storm. The winds blew trees from the ground, rains filled the lands and washed away buildings, and the people became frightened. The leaders of the people began sacrificing their own to the sun god. One day, the master of the warrior was taken to be sacrificed. This gave the warrior a chance to escape. The young warrior returned to our people with this story. That was many elders ago."

A Siknikt elder spoke, "What does this story teach us, friend?"

"It teaches us that Father Sky is mightier than a sun god, that Father Sky protects us, and that we should keep close to the tribe." Everybody sat silently, reflecting on the story until the fire was reduced to embers.

Thinking of traveling down the coast to his home plagued Jesus's brain for several weeks. Could he be so close to home? The story did mention a desert, crocodiles, and pyramids. His heart began to ache for the warmth of his mother's embrace and the guidance of his father.

"I need to go home. I have found great wealth and reward in all places. This place is truly paradise, but my heart aches," Jesus openly spoke with his brothers, The Voice and Healing Dog.

"Then we shall come too. Look at the holes in my hands and feet. If not for you, Jesus, I would have died long ago," Running Dog extended his hands, fingers extended, displaying the holes from his crucifixion.

"Your memory betrays you. I told Troit to leave you." Jesus and Healing Dog grew silent momentarily while looking at the ground.

"What do you think happened to Troit?" Healing Dog softly asked.

"In this life of the next, Odin and Thor have raised him to the clouds and rewarded his loyalty with many riches," Jesus spoke with the authority of a northern scholar of Odin. "He would be proud of us. We continue to serve him well with our knowledge, loyalty, and prosperity."

"Then let us continue to make him proud. Let us find your home. You will be a king of kings with great wealth and many servants," The Voice chimed.

Making their way down the coast was much easier than they had anticipated. They met many tribes and made many trades. The dense leafy forests slowly turned into pines, then swamps. The swamps back into thick forest, then into the hot desert of the gulf. The desert turned into a tall, dark rainforest.

"This is not Egypt," The Voice spoke to Jesus privately.

"I know, but we have traveled far. We will stay a while and see what this place and its people have to offer," Jesus responded. "We need the ground under our feet to refresh our minds and bodies."

Healing Dog approached, "There is a village by that river. We need to stop to fish. Shall we stop here?"

"We should meet the people and see what they have to offer," The Voice answered.

"Tomorrow will be an eventful day," Healing Dog spoke as they ate the last of their fish.

"Yes, we will have a chance to stretch and loosen our limbs. Travel has made us stiff," Jesus was rubbing his calves.

"I need more leaves and flowers for potions and medicine," spoke The Voice. "We may even find a pyramid in this place if the stories are true."

"Look, they line the beach," Jesus pointed at the village.

"The whole village must be waiting for our arrival," added Healing Dog. The people were squatting, staring at the ship. The crowd began to part as the trio made their way ashore. Two elders stood centered in the parted crowd.

"It looks like the welcoming committee is expecting us men. Let's make sure we are not here to be slaves," the tone of Jesus was low and stern.

"Hopefully, they speak a familiar tongue," Healing Dog whispered.

As they ascended the beach, the crowd closed in around them. The elders motioned for them to come and sit at a large hut near the river.

After several hours of using hand gestures, body gestures, and dirt drawings, an agreement culminated. Two village hunters would take the group to a city where a pyramid was located.

"How long shall we wait for our escort," an impatient tone arose from Jesus. "It has been three weeks. We still find ourselves in this mud-hole."

"The way of these people is not our own," soothed Healing Dog. "Remember how they laughed when we fished?"

The Voice laughed, "Yes, even the fish here are different. They hide in the shade. The nets catch none on the sunny side of the boat but drop them on the other side, and our nets are overwhelmed."

"I am sure we would be on our way if we could communicate. It took us until now to exchange names using words," Jesus's frustration had not been tempered. "If we do not leave soon, we will strike out alone."

The next day, when the sun was high in the sky, two villagers motioned for them to follow.

"Here we go, men. Let's find our glory in this place," exhilaration filled the air and Healing Dog's voice.

After two hours of thrashing through the jungle, the trees ended, and a great city met them. In the center was a giant stone, stepped pyramid. The guides seemed very fearful.

Jesus, The Voice, and Healing Dog motioned the guides to enter the city. The guides slowly backed into the forest.

The next moment, a spear entered the eye of one of the guides. Blood and juice spurted as his body convulsed and collapsed.

The remaining guide and the trio ran into the jungle. Heavy footsteps could be heard behind them. They continued to run as the footsteps behind them grew more distant, then stopped.

By the time they had returned, still gasping to the village, they spotted the remaining guide sitting with the village elders.

When the elders spotted the men, the elders yelled while pointing at the group. The trio hunched over and struggled for air while the villagers surrounded them with spears. As they regained their composure, they were escorted to the shoreline. They silently made their way back to their ship, lungs burning, and each with a hand clasping a sword.

CHAPTER VII

The Promised Land

After four years of sailing, four years of trading, four years of surviving brutal attacks, four years of hunger, and four years of the sun beating them into submission, Jesus, Healing Dog, and The Voice arrived on the shores of a village just outside of Alexandria.

"Come, my mother will be serving the evening meal by this time," Jesus pounced upon the shore. "You will be my guests and share in the meal. Let us bring our fish to show our reverence and thanks."

"Have you not tired of fish yet?" Healing Dog had his arms bent with his hands on his hips as he stretched his back.

"The fish are not for us. We will cook them and let my family feast. It is our tradition to give what we can to hungry beggars. There are no hungrier beggars than ourselves," Jesus and the others burst into laughter. "Surely my family will have lamb. Prepare yourselves for fine meat."

"Let's find our feast," The Voice lifted two large fish from the deck. "These won't keep the night. We must consume them while we can."

The dirt felt good under Jesus's feet. There was a soft layer that pleasantly greeted his nose with each step. Children could be heard playing in groups, some nearer than others.

The men drew curious glances from all who passed. As they reached the center of the village, Jesus pointed to a modest building. It had a small courtyard with a donkey.

Jesus began to run and yell, "Father! Father! I have returned. Mother, I have brought guests."

A strange, short, portly man stepped out from the building as Jesus reached the courtyard's edge. Jesus abruptly stopped, frozen.

The man spoke, "You will not find family here. I purchased this home three years ago. The previous owner was stoned. Her daughter lives there." The man pointed to a minuscule building. It was no greater in size than a single bed. A kiln was outside being tended to by a young, attractive woman a couple of years younger than Jesus.

"You there, woman," Jesus yelled.

The woman ran inside the minute home. Jesus walked to the door and turned to his companions. "Cook the fish here. We shall share our bounty."

"Share with a woman who has no room for us?" The Voice protested.

"Share with a member of my tribe who is making soup from sheep hooves." Jesus pointed to a small pot hanging against the kiln. "Woman, we are friends. We have brought you fish so you may dine with us."

"Who are the strange men you bring to my home? I do not entertain such men, such gentiles."

Jesus laughed, "Woman, we are not here to take your body. I used to live there many years ago. I am looking for my father and mother. Do you know where I may find them?"

The woman poked her head through the door. "Which home? I have lived here since I was a child."

"That home," Jesus pointed again. "Tell me your name."

"I am Mary Magdalene. What do people call you?"

"People have called me many things for many years. My father called me Jesus."

"How do I know you speak the truth? How do I know you are not pious and seeking to stone me with your friends?"

"Why would I stone you?"

"You know my sins."

"My sins are far greater. I have sinned enough for ten lifetimes. If I stone you, I must stone myself one hundred times. I have no intention of stoning myself even a single time."

Mary had now come fully across the threshold. "My mother purchased that home when the man who lived there divorced his wife. There was turmoil after their children fell into the ocean and died. The mother grew very sad and wept daily. They tried to have more children, but her sadness prevented it."

"Do you know where they moved?"

Healing Dog and The Voice were turning the fish in the kiln.

"The man moved to Bethlehem. He became a great leader within the faith. The woman disappeared. Nobody knows where she went after she found such disgrace."

"Come, dine with us," Jesus motioned toward the kiln.

"I cannot. I risk my life just by talking to you," her eyes averted to the portly man who watched from across the dirt patch.

"Then we shall leave you a fish so you may dine alone. Do you know where we can find rest this night?"

"Walk this path until you reach a home with two sheep in the courtyard. That will be the butcher. Behind the butcher's home is a small place. Do not yell. Knock at the threshold and tell them I sent you. They will judge if you can have a place to stay this evening."

"That is very peculiar," Jesus responded.

"Have faith, young miracle," the woman's words stung Jesus's ears. "You have shown me a great kindness. The fish you leave me will last for a week."

As they walked, Healing Dog and The Voice spoke while Jesus could not hear. The words of Mary Magdalene haunted Jesus's ears and mind. Memories of his mother's meals, voice, hugs, and teachings raced into his head and danced in his pupils.

"Stay here," Jesus pointed to the wall outside the courtyard. "We do not want to startle whoever may live here. We are uninvited guests."

"And if they do not take kindly to you encroaching on their property?" The Voice pointed at Jesus's sword.

"We do not need these here. Have faith," Jesus removed his sword and placed it on the wall as he entered the courtyard.

"Jesus! Jesus! Have you lost your mind?" Healing Dog was shouting in a whisper.

Jesus turned and motioned the men to be silent as he reached the threshold. The sun had nearly retreated into pinks, reds, and oranges. The clay wall was warm as Jesus tapped his closed fist against it. "Mary Magdalene has sent me to this place. Is there room for me and my companions to rest?"

"Come in and sit, traveler," the melodic sound delighted Jesus's ears. "All of you must come and sit."

Jesus turned and waved for his friends to join. The inside was dimly lit by a small oil lamp sitting on the table. Looking around, they could see two doors leading to the blackness of rooms containing no windows.

"Shall we wait our entire lives," Healing Dog was growing impatient with exhaustion.

"Place your coin on the table. We shall relieve the stress of your journeys, noble warriors," a magnificent, olive-skinned woman entered the room. Her supple, bare breasts were an unexpected site. "The gentiles will cost five extra coins. Based on your exotic garbs, this is a very fair price."

"You hold immense beauty. Cleopatra herself would be jealous," Jesus's mouth was dry from the shock, "But we are not here to pay for your entertainment."

The woman ran back into the blackness as two men with swords emerged.

"No!" Yelled a woman as she dove from the other room. She landed at Jesus's feet and held her hands upward, defending from the swords.

"Mother?" Jesus's question trembled.

"My son," She turned, clenched Jesus with the grip of a bear. "How are you here? Joseph said Daniel fell into the sea. You tried to save him. He said your body was lost to sharks."

The men with swords were now looking out the door, checking to see if anyone had seen the men enter the home.

"Bring us wine. My son has returned home. We still have lamb from dinner. Let my son and his friends feast."

"Mother, we brought fish," the room was a calamity with excitement, food preparation, and talking.

The woman who had been scantily clad and one of the men retired first, then the other sword holder, then Jesus's compatriates. Jesus and his mother spoke nearly until the sun rose.

The following day came, and Jesus assisted his mother in all ways. There was no task too womanly to keep Jesus from his mother's side. Mary told Jesus about how Joseph had divorced her and how she lived as a beggar in the streets. She had stolen from the trough of pigs. She was going to die a poor beggar until the prostitutes took pity on her. She served the prostitutes. She prepared every meal, made all the clothes, and tended to their market needs. They could not bring their money to market in fear of being stoned, but she could.

Healing Dog and The Voice saw great opportunity in this land. Many ailments were very easy to cure. They used their knowledge of teas, lotions, and medicines to make a healthy profit.

Jesus's trio were the only men in the land who would care for the medical needs of the prostitutes. They did it in secret, so neither they nor the women risked death.

After a couple of months with his mother, Jesus's desire to travel resurfaced. As did his wanting to find his father.

The group reached Bethlehem in the middle of the day. The journey had taken much longer than expected because Jesus's mother was not as young as she once was. They found a place to rest in the center of town.

The rooster just began to crow when Jesus reached the temple. Beggars littered the streets while men adorned in brightly colored robes decorated with gold and silver entered the temple. One of the robed men kicked a dirty pile of rag-covered bones before entering the temple.

Jesus ascended the stairs and entered. He approached one of the men, "I am looking for Joseph, the father of Daniel and Jesus."

The man turned and walked away. Jesus tried another man with the same question. The man provided the same response. Jesus tried a third man and received the same response. A group of men speaking nearby overheard the pleading.

One of the men approached Jesus, "Why do you think this 'Joseph' is here? Why do you ask for him?" As the two men locked eyes, the man stepped back and gasped. Jesus opened his arms to embrace the man but was met with a hard shove. Jesus fell to the floor. "You are not worthy of touching me, peasant. For your insolence, god has commanded me to cast you out of the temple," the man yelled. A crowd began to gather. "You and your demonic ways are cast out of this place. Be removed from my sight." Men standing around grabbed Jesus and lifted him.

"Father, you know who I am."

"You have no father here, demon! You have sinned against this place and god! Cast him and his wicked ways out of this place!"

Jesus tumbled down the steps as men kicked and beat him. "Father, why have you forsaken me," Jesus screamed through his tears and the flurry of fists.

"Get back! Get back!" Healing Dog and The Voice ran to Jesus with their swords drawn.

"Sheath your swords and take me from this place," Jesus screamed. As they departed, Jesus saw Joseph standing atop the temple steps. Joseph was silently watching them leave, anger draped across his entire being.

"Come, Jesus, we do not need the temples of holy men. We will find glory and wealth in the healing we provide to the people," Healing Dog tried to comfort as he bore the weight of Jesus's battered, bleeding body.

"And, as we heal people in this life, we will surely be rewarded in the next. This life is meant for us to earn a life as kings in the next," The Voice offered the forsaken friend.

"Then let us aspire to live in the house of Father Sky as doves in our next life. In Father's house, the dove has no quarrels or hardships," Jesus finished as he curbed his tears.

www.ingramcontent.com/pod-product-compliance
Lightning Source LLC
Chambersburg PA
CBHW030406160726
47992CB00007B/2984